The Virtual Tutor

by Elaine Roche-Tombee
illustrated by Frank Carpenter

Chapters

Harcourt

Orlando   Boston   Dallas   Chicago   San Diego

Visit *The Learning Site!*

www.harcourtschool.com

Who Wants Pizza?

I was just sitting there in math class, minding my own business. So why did the teacher have to pick on me?

"This one's for you, Amalia!" said Mr. Baer. How could he sound so cheerful when he was talking about a math problem? "Listen carefully. I've got three-fourths of a pizza, and I divide it into six equal slices. What fraction of a pizza is each slice?"

"Uh…" I was in a panic. I started to draw a pizza and slice it with my pencil, but it quickly became a jumble of crossed lines. Frantically I worked out the numbers. Three-fourths divided by six…

"Four and a half?" I whispered.

"Four and a half of a pizza?" said Mr. Baer.

I was bombarded with giggles from the class.

Mr. Baer sighed a little and looked around the class. "Brian, what answer do you get?"

Of course, Brian didn't even need to pick up his pencil. He had done the problem in his head!

"It's one-eighth," he said with a little smile.

Mr. Baer beamed at him. "That's right!" Then he looked at me out of the corner of his eye and shook his head. He tried to hide it, but I saw him.

"That was embarrassing," I told my friends after school. We were at Leone's—eating a real pizza—Devon, Fito, Brian, and I. "I mean, dividing up three-fourths of a pizza and coming up with four and a half slices?"

"Maybe you need a tutor," Devon said helpfully.

"No, I'm good at math," I said. At least I had been until division of fractions reared its ugly head.

"There's no shame in admitting you need help," said Fito as he cast an imaginary fishing line. Fito is of the opinion that any moment not spent fishing is a waste of time. Weird.

"I *don't* need help," I said, too loudly. "I made a mistake, that's all. Listen, could we not talk about math anymore?"

"Sure," said Brian, wolfing down his last bite of pizza. "I'm late for my saxophone lesson anyway."

"And I've got to get over to the ice-skating rink," Devon said. She threw a few dollars down and flung her skates over her shoulder. "See you tomorrow, guys."

Help, Please

I did need help. I just didn't want a barrage of it from all sides. I was being bombarded with good intentions, but I was still very confused.

There had to be some simple clue that would help me connect division of fractions to the real world. If pizza wouldn't do it, then what would?

That evening, after struggling with my math homework, I went online. A short break to check my messages was just what I needed.

I had a few online pen pals. I didn't know many of their real names, and we would probably never meet. We all went by screen names. I love music, so I use the name "noteworthy." Get it?

The modem hissed and whistled. The icons flashed. I had e-mail.

Dear Noteworthy,

You need to take the reciprocal of the divisor and THEN multiply. Think about how the numbers make sense. You're not sharing 3/4 of a pizza with 1/6 of a friend. You're dividing it 6 ways. That means you must end up with a share that's less than 3/4.

The message was not signed, but there was a return address: piscator@cnet.com.

There was an attached file. That's always interesting.
Normally, I don't open attachments from strangers. Some
joker could trash your files with a virus.

There has been quite a barrage of viruses in recent
years. In fact, one nearly wiped out all the information
stored on the computers at my mom's office. No one
had even known the virus was there until it wormed its
way through most of the company files. What a mess!

I knew Mom would be upset if I let a virus into our home computer. But piscator@cnet.com was no stranger. Somehow I knew it was Devon, Fito, or Brian. Apparently, I am better at guessing who sent me e-mail than I am at multiplying and dividing fractions.

The attachment turned out to be a neat little interactive pizza graphic that made the problem perfectly clear. Someone had gone to a lot of trouble to help me.

Mysterious Messages

Devon, Fito, or Brian could have done it. They were all in the computer club. Devon had designed the school's web site. Fito was always making up computer games, most of which involved fishing. And Brian—well, when the computer in the school office crashed, Brian had brought it back online.

At school the next day, none of them would admit to sending the message. They all pretended they didn't know what I was talking about. In math I bombed again.

This time we had to divide *by* fractions.

"You've got a cookie recipe that calls for one and a third cups of sugar," Mr. Baer said. "You only have two-thirds of a cup of sugar. What fraction of the recipe can you make?"

"Why can't you go to the store and buy more sugar?" That was Tim, the class clown.

"The stores are closed," said Mr. Baer. "Amalia?"

I knew you had to convert the mixed number to thirds and divide, but what did you divide by what?

"Two?" I answered.

"Two what?"

"Two cups of sugar?"

That evening I turned on my modem again to see if there was any help out there for me. Piscator had sent another transmission. This one was posted on the school's website.

"You have to write mixed numbers as fractions. Then you have to figure out which fraction is the divisor. Then you have to think! You've got LESS than the amount of sugar you need for one recipe. How can your answer turn out to be MORE than one recipe?"

The problem was explained using pizza icons. I guess piscator hadn't wanted to redo the graphics. I had no trouble seeing how you would divide two-thirds of a pizza among one and a third people. Maybe it was because I was feeling I had about one-third of a brain.

The Mystery Continues

It went on like that all week. Each day, piscator left a little interactive graphic transmission that made the math clear. By the end of the week, I was dividing fractions with confidence—even out loud in class.

"You're dividing eight and one-fourth by one and a half," I explained. "Eight and one-fourth is thirty-three fourths. One and a half is three halves. You multiply by the reciprocal, which is two-thirds…"

I also remembered my English skills. When you meet a new and strange word, there's a place you can go to get better acquainted. The dictionary didn't help with my math, but it did clear up a mystery.

Mr. Baer gave us a test on Friday. I was sure I had gotten an A. After school I went to Leone's with Devon, Fito, and Brian again.

"I aced that test!" I told them. "I know I did!"

I caught Devon sneaking a glance at the boys. Fito was smiling in a strange way. Of course, for him that was not unusual.

"Well, that's good," Brian said. "Glad to know you're not going to fail math."

"I was *never* going to *fail*," I retorted. "But it was nice to get help. Thanks, piscator." I studied the slice of pizza in my hand to avoid looking at anyone.

"Who are you talking to?" Devon asked.

"Oh, I think all three of you know," I said. I looked at each of them in turn. They were all fighting not to smile. "But," I added, "the one who's been sending those messages is Fito."

"Nope!" he insisted. "It's not me! I don't know a thing about fractions."

"Yes, it is you!" I said. "The reason I know that is because *piscator* means 'fisher,' and fishing is your favorite hobby."

"Have another five-fifths of a slice," said Fito with a big grin.